8132

CHO

Oink and Pearl

Chorao, Kay

An I CAN READ Book

Oink
and
Pearl

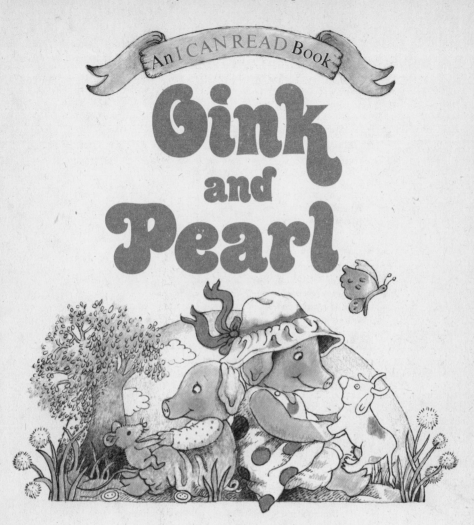

Kay Chorao

Harper & Row, Publishers

This book is a presentation of Weekly Reader Books.
Weekly Reader Books offers book clubs for children from
preschool through junior high school.

For further information write to:
Weekly Reader Books
1250 Fairwood Ave.
Columbus, Ohio 43216

Library of Congress Cataloging in Publication Data
Chorao, Kay.
    Oink and Pearl.

    (An I can read book)
    Summary: Presents the adventures of two piglets,
Pearl and her little brother Oink.
    [1. Brothers and sisters—Fiction. 2. Pigs—Fiction]
I. Title. II. Series: I can read book.
PZ7.C4463Oi 1981   [E]   80-8439
ISBN 0-06-021272-1   AACR2
ISBN 0-06-021273-X (lib. bdg.)

Contents

JUMP ROPE

Pearl watched Oink

put a bib on Mouse.

"I wish I had a big sister,"

she said.

"Why do you play

with that silly doll?"

Oink did not answer.

"*Now* what are you doing?"

she asked.

"Feeding Mouse his cookie,"

said Oink.

"Dolls do not eat buttons,"

said Pearl.

"It is not a doll.

It is Mouse.

And this is not a button.

It is a cookie," said Oink.

"This is awful," shouted Pearl.

She jumped up

and looked out the window.

"A big sister would jump rope
with me," said Pearl.

"You can play with me,"
said Oink.

"Never!" said Pearl.

"All you do
is play with that silly doll."

"Mouse is not silly,"
whispered Oink.

8

Pearl picked up her jump rope.

"A big sister

would teach me jumping songs.

And if I fell,

she would bandage my knee."

Oink was not listening.

He was tucking Mouse in bed.

9

"Good-by!" shouted Pearl.

"Shhh, Mouse is sleeping,"

said Oink.

Pearl slammed the door.

She ran down the stairs.

She ran under the trees.

She found Nellie and Agnes

jumping rope.

"I can jump too," said Pearl.

Pearl jumped her rope.

"That is baby jumping," said Agnes.

"Let's see you jump two ropes,"
said Nellie.

Nellie and Agnes swung the ropes
in two big circles.

12

The ropes buzzed through the air.

They buzzed fast,

like mosquitos.

Pearl jumped between the ropes.

She tried hard.

13

But the ropes got stuck

in her feet.

Pearl crashed on her head.

"Ouch," she cried.

"Only babies cry," said Nellie.

"Crybabies," said Agnes.

Pearl covered her eyes.

"I am not crying," she said.

But her head hurt.

Pearl ran home,

back under the trees,

back up the stairs.

"Do not cry," said Oink.

"I will make the hurt go away."

He put a cool cloth

on Pearl's head.

He got a hankie

so she could blow her nose.

He pulled back the cover

on his bed.

Pearl closed her eyes.

Oink pulled the cover

over his sister

and sang Mouse's favorite song

in a very soft voice.

Little mouse crackers

in the sky.

Moon nibbles one,

and so do I.

Little mouse crackers

up so high,

dancing with stars

who tumble by.

Pearl opened one eye.

"Mouse can nap with me,"

she whispered.

She opened her other eye.

"But do not expect me

to kiss him good night."

19

FISH

One hot day

Pearl found Oink

in the toolshed.

He was dusting

an old fishing pole.

"Look what I found,"

he squealed.

"We can take the rowboat

and catch a pile of fish."

"No way," said Pearl.

Oink picked up the fishing pole

and headed for the pond.

"Wait," called Pearl.

"You need worms for bait."

"I do?" asked Oink.

"Of course," said Pearl.

So they dug for worms.

Oink watched them wiggle

in the can.

"They are nice," he said.

"Ugh," said Pearl.

The rowboat was tied to a tree.

Oink pulled at the rope.

"It is stuck," he cried.

"Once, my jump rope

got like this," said Pearl.

She worked and worked

until the rope came loose.

"Hop in," she said.

They rowed

to the middle

of the pond.

Oink dropped his fishing line

into the water.

"Oink," Pearl said,

"you forgot the bait."

Oink looked at the worms.

"Do we have to?" he asked.

"I will do it," said Pearl.

Oink closed his eyes

while Pearl put a worm

on the hook.

They sat a long time

with the line in the water.

They sat and sat.

The sun grew hotter and hotter.

"This is fun," said Oink.

"It is very boring," said Pearl.

Suddenly, Oink felt something

tug at his hook.

He pulled his line.

A huge fish wiggled

and twisted on it.

"Look, Pearl," cried Oink.

28

"I caught a fish!

Now what do I do?"

"Hang on tight,"

yelled Pearl.

She pulled the fish

into the boat.

29

Oink stared at it.

He had never seen a fish

so close.

"His eyes are meaner

than a snake's eyes,"

he whispered.

"His teeth are sharper

than Papa's saw.

His mouth is bigger

than Mama's spaghetti pot."

Oink backed away so fast

that he rocked the boat.

It tipped left.

Then it tipped right.

"Watch out!" cried Pearl.

She caught Oink just in time.

The fish jumped off the hook

and back into the water.

"Good-by, fish," whispered Oink.

Oink and Pearl

watched the fish swim away.

Now the water was as smooth

as a green mirror.

"I caught a fish," said Oink.

"And I caught you," said Pearl.

Oink watched his face

and Pearl's face

on the mirror

of green water.

"I really caught a fish,"

he whispered.

CHOROCOLATE CAKE

One day Pearl got a letter.

It said,

Dear Pearl,

We are sorry we made you fall on your head.

Please come to our garden party at three o'clock.

We will have chocolate cake.
Bring a doll.
Bring Oink too.

Yours truly,
Agnes and Nellie

"I am not going," said Pearl.

"But they want to be friends,"

said Oink.

"Pooh," said Pearl.

"Anyway, it looks like rain."

"But they will have

CHOCOLATE CAKE!" said Oink.

"Hummmm," said Pearl.

"Maybe we will go.

Just for a little while."

"Yum," said Oink.

At three o'clock,

Oink and Pearl left their house.

"It still looks like rain,"

grumbled Pearl.

A party table

was set under the trees.

Balloons

were tied to the chairs.

Nellie and Agnes were there.

So were the twins,

Tina and Teddy.

Everyone held a doll.

"Is that your doll?" asked Nellie.

"Yes, his name is Rex,"

said Pearl.

"Oh," said Nellie.

"Hummm," said Agnes.

Pearl could tell

they did not like Rex.

"Now we will all sit down

and I will pour tea," said Agnes.

"I will serve cake," said Nellie.

"But there is no cake,"

wailed Oink.

"It is pretend cake," said Agnes.

"I want real chocolate cake,"

cried Oink.

"Me too," cried Tina.

"Me three," cried Teddy.

"Let's go home," said Oink.

"But we bought balloons,"

said Nellie.

44

"And we decorated the table,"

said Agnes.

"I think it is going to get wet,

and so are we," said Pearl.

Raindrops fell on the balloons.

PLOP PLOPPITY-PLOP

They fell faster and faster.

"My party dress is ruined,"
cried Agnes.

"Mine too," wailed Nellie.

"So are your dolly dresses,"
said Tina.

She giggled.

Oink and Pearl giggled too.

"Go home!" yelled Nellie.

"Good-by!" cried Pearl.

"And take that dumb doll,"

yelled Agnes.

"Who wants to stay, anyway?"

said Oink.

"Let's have a MUD party!"

yelled Pearl.

Oink and Pearl

and Tina and Teddy

jumped in the mud.

"Let's make a big mud

CHOCOLATE CAKE," squealed Oink.

"Yippee," they all yelled.

It was so much fun

even Nellie and Agnes jumped in.

AUNTIE MIN

Auntie Min was coming to visit.

"I hope Auntie Min

will stay and stay," sang Pearl.

"I hate company," grumbled Oink.

"I have to dress up

and keep my room neat."

"Last time Auntie Min came,

she pushed me

on the swing

and held me high

to touch the leaves,"

said Pearl.

"I do not remember,"

said Oink.

"You were not born yet,"

said Pearl.

The bell rang.

Pearl ran to the door.

"Hello, Auntie Min,

look how big I am."

"My, my," said Auntie Min.

She kissed Pearl.

Then she kissed Oink.

Oink wiped his cheek

where Auntie Min kissed him.

"Now let me look

at our precious baby,"

said Auntie Min.

"I can jump rope," said Pearl.

"Very nice, Pearl.

Come, Oink, sit on Auntie's lap,"

said Auntie Min.

"And I make up poems,"

said Pearl.

"Yes, dear.

Now, Oink,

watch Auntie

do a trick

with a hankie."

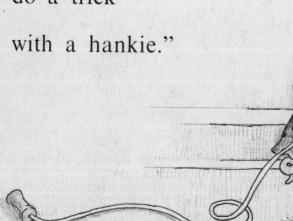

"I could bash him," thought Pearl.

Auntie Min showed Oink

how to fold a hankie

into sleeping babies.

"You see,

my little sweetmeat?"

said Auntie Min.

She kissed Oink again.

Oink wiped his cheek

and slid off Auntie's lap.

"I could bop that Oink,"

thought Pearl.

At dinner,

Oink pushed a pea off his plate.

Auntie Min saw it.

She winked at Oink.

"I hated peas

when I was little, too,"

she whispered.

Pearl stuck a fork

into two of her peas.

"I will get him," she thought.

57

That night,

Pearl came up behind Oink.

"NOW I will bop him,"

Pearl thought.

Pearl raised her pillow

higher and higher.

Just then,

Oink turned around.

He looked mad.

He looked as mad

as Pearl felt.

"I am *not* a precious baby,"

he cried.

"I know,"

said Pearl in surprise.

"And I am not a sweetmeat.

She made me look silly,"

cried Oink.

"She did?" said Pearl.

"Nellie was looking

in our window.

She was laughing.

Now she will tell everyone

that I am a baby."

Oink sniffed.

"I wish I was big, like you."

"You do?" said Pearl.

Oink nodded.

"Don't worry.

I will not let Nellie tease you,"

said Pearl.

"I will bop her

if she does."

Pearl put her arm

around Oink.

"Sometimes I wish I was little,

like you," she whispered.

"You do?" said Oink.

"Sometimes," said Pearl, yawning.

Oink yawned too.

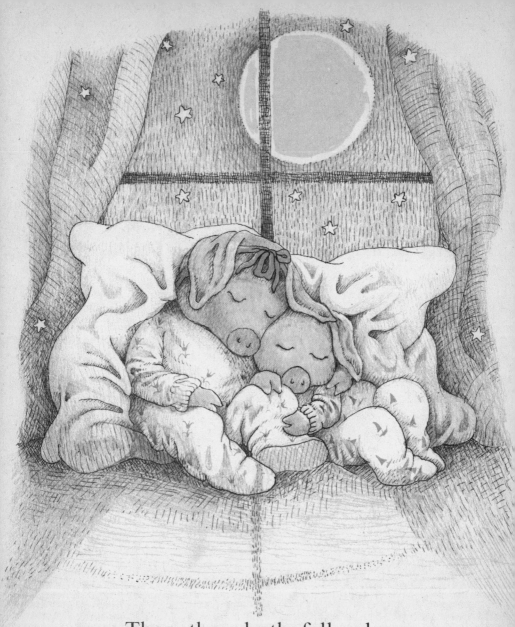

Then they both fell asleep

on Pearl's pillow.